D7

PHILIP FRAĊASSI

A NOVELETTE

Shortwave

D7

Philip Fracassi

SHORTWAVE

Cover and interior design by Alan Lastufka.

First Edition published May 2025.

10 9 8 7 6 5 4 3 2 1

ISBN 978-1-959565-62-8 (Paperback)
ISBN 978-1-959565-63-5 (eBook)

For Chris and Menaka

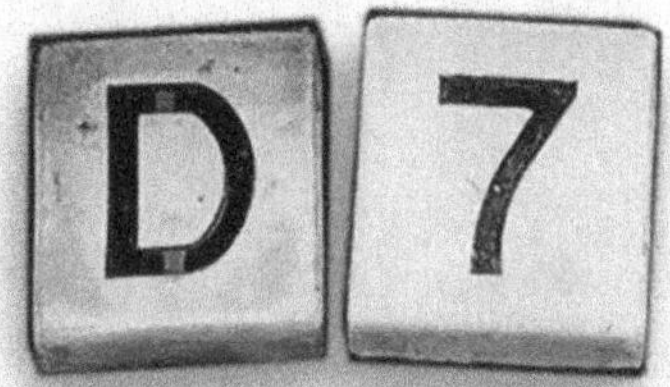
D 7

Chapter One

"Nightcap?"

Dinner had been wildly unsatisfying for them both, and while they weren't exactly in the middle of nowhere, they were far from anything familiar. And yet, here they were, stuck between two pinpoints of the United States—one on the West Coast and one on the East—a muddled middle-of-nowhere piece of the country where your late-night options were a diner with slippery floors and greasy tables (and greasier cheeseburgers, as they'd discovered), or nothing at all.

The hotel they'd booked for the night was fine, but they were both eager to get back on the open road come morning and leave this funky little patch of mid-south in the rearview mirror. If everything went to plan, in two days they'd be pulling into the driveway of their new home in western Pennsylvania, leaving behind the smog and traffic and overpopulation of Los Angeles for three acres of woodland and a house big enough to hold a family of four (which was the long-term plan, after all).

Sitting in the passenger seat, however, Diane is unnerved.

Driving back to the hotel through the same twisting, unfamiliar roads at night feels a lot different than driving them a couple hours ago. At least then the sun was still setting and you could see land all around, giving you a sense of where you were at and where you were headed. Now she feels as if they're driving through outer space, the night around them so dense it seems to douse the headlight beams, the darkness itself eagerly pressing against the car windows, wanting inside.

"Did the hotel have a bar? I didn't notice."

Paul shrugs. "Doubtful. Looked like the only employee in the evenings was the kid who checked us in. But maybe we can find a bar out here. . . . what's the GPS say?"

"I don't want to start driving around blindly," she says, feeling sluggish and full after the diner meal. "This area is weird."

"Yeah. . . maybe we'll just raid the mini bar."

"I don't recall seeing a mini bar either," she says with a chuckle. "But I do think I want to get back."

"Agreed," Paul says. "Is this the turn?"

"Uh. . ." Diane taps the car's touchscreen, opens the GPS map. "Shit, it doesn't even show this as a road."

"Well, that can't be good."

"No, it's not. I think you better turn around and go back. . . here, see?" She points to the GPS screen, where the curvy black line of known road is slowly receding behind the blue dot of their vehicle, which seems to have come untethered from reality and now floats freely in an obscene sea of green.

"I could have sworn this was the turn. . ."

"Paul, it's pitch black out there. I can't see any landmarks at all." Diane scans the surrounding darkness, but sees nothing but dense forest encroaching the narrow road, a blank black sky hovering above.

"At least it's not raining?"

"Paul, I'm—"

"Hey, look."

Paul points at something ahead. Diane leans forward, notices a soft white light coming from the side of the road a little ways off, just past a wall of tall trees. As they drive closer, the shoulders of the road widen, the forest retreats, and the source of light comes into view.

"That's not the hotel."

"Duh," he says, sitting up eagerly. "But it might be a bar."

"A biker bar, maybe."

"Even cooler!"

"Paul..."

"Let's just... let's just see."

As the building comes into full view, Diane realizes (with a mixture of relief and misgivings) that it is indeed a bar. By the looks of it a honky-tonk. The exterior is all dark, wide wood board and batten siding, neon-splashed tinted windows, and honest-to-God wagon wheels on either side of the porch entrance.

Surprisingly, there's a large gravel parking lot near capacity.

Above the porch roof, painted in bold (if weathered) white letters that span the entire length of the building, are the words: HAPPY'S BAR & GRILL.

"Look at this!" Paul says, obviously thrilled with the discovery. "And not a single motorcycle in the lot. Just good ole folks having a good ole time. Hell, I bet there's even a band playing."

"Paul..."

"Bar *and* grill? Honey, we could have eaten here. I bet the burgers are the best in the state."

"Paul, I'm tired."

"One drink," he says, parking the hybrid cross-over between two mud-spattered pickup trucks.

"One drink, and we go back to the hotel. I just want to, you know, experience different stuff. Take in some of the local color."

Diane sighs. "Fine. One drink. But listen, band or no band. . ." she says as she pops the door open and steps into the cold night.

"What?"

"No dancing."

The couple step up onto the broad, wood-planked porch, then pause in front of the closed front door to study a sign tacked to its face:

NO GUNS
NO KNIVES
NO FIGHTING

Diane gives Paul a sidelong glance, which he matches.

"Darn it, honey," she says sweetly, "we better leave the AR-15 in the trunk."

"Like hell I am," Paul says gruffly, hands on hips. "This is America, dammit."

Diane laughs, but neither of them lifts a hand toward the door, as if there was an invisible barrier between them and whatever waited inside, a vibrating membrane of resistance that would take a concerted effort to pass through.

"They're open, right?"

Paul nods. "I hear music. And the cars. . ." he adds lamely, motioning to the full lot of vehicles behind them.

"Sure, of course."

Abruptly, as if pulling off a Band-Aid, Diane steps forward, reaches for the large handle, and pulls.

The door opens without resistance. Warm light spills over their bodies and onto the surrounding porch. Something soulful and rhythmic—old electric blues in the vein of Stevie Ray Vaughan or Jeff Beck—vibrates the air around them, beckons them inside.

Paul and Diane share one more—one last— quick look.

This is okay, right?

Then Paul shrugs, puts his hand on the small of his wife's back, and together they walk into the bar, into the light, into the music.

Behind them, the door swings silently closed. . . and locks.

Chapter Two

FOR BETTER OR WORSE, the interior of Happy's Bar and Grill is almost, to a tee, what Diane had expected. There's a long, scuffed oak bar running along one side, a main dining area scattered with four-top tables, and a row of dark booths along the opposite wall. Just beyond all that is a generous dance floor—*good enough for some two-steppin'*, she thinks—that includes a small stage shoved into one corner. To the left of the dance floor is a darkened hallway that leads deeper into the building, most likely to GUYS and GALS restrooms. The entire place is a hodgepodge of

different shades and patterns of wood: the weathered barn plank floors (coffee brown—likely from
years of being trod upon), the long oak bar (a
bright maple color, at least where it isn't stained),
and the shellacked-to-hell pine four tops (wal-
nut). Old-timey chandeliers litter the ceiling,
swayed gently by the current modern black ceiling
fans—all of which spin lazily, just enough to keep
the air from getting overly stuffy.

Not too shabby, Diane thinks, pleased not to be
disappointed by the place. *Hell, this might even
be fun.*

The place, as they had already figured out
based on the cars in the lot, is indeed full.

Nearly every booth and table taken.

So why's it so damn quiet?

*There's no laughing or yelling. No drunken hoots.
No conversation. . .*

Just. . . quiet.

Except for that music, Diane thinks, looking
around for the source.

And that's when she sees it.

Hunched along the rear wall of the dance floor,
and facing the rest of the restaurant like a
watchful eye—glowing in bright, pulsing reds,
greens, and yellows, and playing that old electric
bluesy rock 'n roll, as if it was force-feeding the
goddamn place a bellyful of good times—is a
jukebox.

Diane feels a tug at her elbow and turns to see Paul staring straight ahead, his mouth clamped into a frown.

"What?"

He looks at her, then leans close and whispers. "I think we're intruding."

Diane's brief, brewing joy goes from boil to simmer, and she turns to examine the bar's interior once more, and suddenly—shockingly—realizes what he's referring to.

Everyone is looking at them.

Everyone.

Every table, every chair, every barstool, every booth. Even the bartender is staring, his mouth slightly open in surprise, as if two aliens from outer space, green-skinned and tentacle-armed, had just strolled into the place.

Diane also notices there are no bustling waitresses carrying trays of food, no bussers clearing tables, and no fresh drinks being served at the bar.

The dance floor is empty.

Everyone—every single person—is sitting at a table, stool, or booth, and simply. . .

Staring at them.

Diane leans toward her husband, eyes locked on the strange crowd. "Should we leave?"

Paul nods. "Abso-fucking-lutely."

They both take a small step backward. Paul lifts a hand, waves. "Sorry to have bothered you," he says, his voice easily carrying over the sound of the jukebox.

Diane, feeling sick with anxiety, turns around and presses her hands against the door's push-handle. It drops a few inches, but the door doesn't release.

She pushes again, harder.

"Shit."

Paul is next to her. "Let me..."

He slams his hands into the handle. Nothing. He throws a hip into the door...

"That won't open," a man's deep voice rumbles from somewhere behind them. "Not now, anyway," he adds, and a quiet, rippling murmur spreads across the room.

Folks nod in agreement.

"We shoulda made a run for it!" another man yells angrily. "I told you someone else would come."

"Oh, shut your trap, Harold," a woman snaps back.

Paul spins around, eyes the crowd warily. "Hey... I don't know what's..."

He holds up his hands, as if warding off an invisible threat.

But no one has so much as shifted a chair. No one has stood, or approached them. If anything, Diane thinks, the bartender has taken a step further away.

"Once it's locked, it's locked," a woman from a nearby booth says, disappointment, or perhaps sadness, in her voice.

"And don't bother with the windows, or the kitchen door, or the emergency exit by the johns," a third, much younger, man says. He's seated at a table with a pretty girl; both wearing shorts and T-shirts, as if they'd arrived in the middle of a hot afternoon instead of the dead of a brittle, cold night. "None of it opens," he adds with a heavy sigh and a slow shake of his head. "No matter what you do."

He says this last part with such resigned despair that Diane feels the urge to go to the young man and give him a hug.

Paul, meanwhile, takes a couple steps forward, scrutinizing all the faces that are watching them. Finally, he settles on the bartender, a round-bellied man in jeans and a flannel, with a scraggly beard and a mop of black hair above wide brown eyes.

Everyone in this place could use a razor, Diane thinks, not meaning to be unkind, but unable to help noticing the facial hair on nearly all the men; the scraggly, messy hair of many of the women.

"Look, what's this all about?" Paul asks the bartender, singling him out. "Come on, man. We want to leave now."

"You and everyone else," a young woman yells

from a far corner of the room, and there's a loud
murmur among the crowd—this time the general
response sounds less like simple agreement and
more like bitter amusement.

A few people even chuckle.

Someone else weeps.

Chapter Three

"HERE YA GO, FOLKS!" a thin, long-faced man near the middle of the room says, gesturing toward Paul and Diane. "I got a table for ya." He cackles a bit and wipes theatrically at a nearby table and its adjacent chair seats with a bare hand. "Last one, I think, so better get it before it's taken!"

"Jesus, John," the woman next to the long-faced man says. "Don't be cruel."

He spins toward her—presumably his wife, or his date—and she shrinks back. "I ain't being mean!" he nearly screams. "I'm being mother-fucking helpful!"

"Okay. . ." she says, eyes filling with tears.

"Take it easy, fella," another man says from a couple tables over, arms thick as pythons beneath a tight black T-shirt. "No need to make things worse."

The big man stands, faces Paul and Diane, and nods toward the empty table. "But he's right. You should take a seat if you can. We're nearly out of chairs, and the floor. . . well, I think a chair is better."

Paul nods slowly. "Sure. . . anything is better than the floor, of course." He gives Diane a *what the hell is this* look, but she only shakes her head.

As they walk toward the lone empty table, skirting between the backs and shoulders of the other patrons, Diane notices a few odd things— well, *odder* things—in regards to the people seated all around them.

For one, she notes that no one has food. There are no half-eaten steaks, bowls of melting ice cream; no cheeseburgers with French fries. . . no plates at all.

Even stranger, there are no drinks. Well, there're drinks, but not. . . *drinks.*

At every table, every person seated has a glass of water in front of them. A few sip from their glasses as Paul and Diane pass by. But there are no beers, no cocktails, no whiskeys or gin and tonics. Just. . . water.

As Paul pulls out her chair, it's only then she realizes the one other thing that's been bothering her, something she hadn't been able to fully put her finger on until she got close enough.

Everyone in this room looks completely, undeniably... exhausted.

Even more? They stink. The whole room smells of unwashed bodies, as if she and her husband had stumbled into a locker room filled with hockey players straight after a double-overtime game.

After they sit down, Diane has to fight the urge to tuck her chin and give her own pits a quick sniff, but then sees the bartender walking toward them, looking haggard and tired, carrying two pint glasses filled with water.

He sets one down in front of each of them, wipes his hands on his red flannel shirt. "All we got left is tap, but it's okay to drink," he says. "I'll show you where the sink is, back behind the bar. When those glasses are empty, you'll have to refill your own." Sheepishly, he adds: "I have a little pride left, so I always bring the first round myself. It's still my place, damn it, and well. . . I. . . ." He trails off, as if not knowing what it means that it's his place, or if such a thing even matters in the scheme of things.

"You're Happy?" Diane asks, feeling a wave of sympathy for these people.

"Yeah," he answers. "Welcome, I guess."

"Can we get a couple beers?" Paul asks. "Budweiser is fine."

Happy squints at Paul strangely, as if he was

speaking a foreign language. "You, uh. . . you don't want beer, friend. Drink that water." He leans in close, so close that Paul fights not to pull back from the stench of the man's body, his breath. "But if you want something hard, just help yourself. On the house."

"What about food?" Diane asks. She isn't hungry, but wants to understand what's happening here, why everything is so strange.

"Rationing," he says matter-of-factly, as if it almost went without saying. "You'll get your portion. . ."

"Less food for us," someone says from the far end of the bar, interrupting their conversation.

Happy turns, hands wringing. "It ain't their fault!" he snaps. He looks around the room. "And I'll treat them the same as any one of you."

Many folks nod, others only stare, blank-eyed, uncaring.

"Anyway," he says, turning his attention back to Paul and Diane. "It'll likely be starting up again soon, so I better go rest my feet."

As Happy walks away, Paul turns in his chair, calling after him. "Starting?"

But Happy doesn't answer. He shuffles further back behind the long oak bar and sits himself down on a stool, head bowed, as if taking a nap.

The song on the jukebox fades away, and for the time it takes to inhale a breath, a dead silence settles over the bar. Diane looks around and notices that everyone is staring at the jukebox. As if waiting to find out what the next song is. . .

Paul and Diane, without understanding why, also turn and look at the machine.

Diane imagines the jukebox as a large, multi-colored face, its lone eye a broad window showing a hundred black records. A darting mechanical arm flitters among them, sorting, choosing. Just below the eye are rows of song titles, each one given a code that you enter to play a particular record. And, below that, two rows of glowing buttons—dimly lit letters and numbers that could easily be mistaken for a grinning mouth of yellow teeth.

As they all watch, the machine begins to change the record, even though no one has gone anywhere near the thing.

Someone must have paid for multiple songs, Diane thinks, as the machine readies to play a new record.

Suddenly, music *bursts* from the jukebox's grilled speakers, so shockingly loud that Diane gasps and Paul jerks back as if slapped. The music seems to come from all around them, the bass beats so heavy Diane feels the vibrations in her skull.

Paul looks at her, wide-eyed.

"They must have hidden speakers?" Diane says, nearly yelling to make herself heard over the noise. . . over the song.

And just what the hell song is this, anyway? she thinks, unable to place the rockabilly tune. She has to admit it's catchy, despite the insane volume at which it's being played—easily ten times as loud as the previous song they'd heard.

Around them, people begin to rise from the tables, and the room fills with the sounds of scraping chairs and shuffling feet as the patrons move toward the dance floor.

"Popular song?" Paul says, eyeing the people as they walk by.

The dance floor begins to fill up, and still more patrons continue to stand and make their way forward.

"I guess so," Diane says with a small laugh, but something makes her uneasy about the way they're all herding forward.

And this song. . . there's something tickling my brain. . . how do I know this song?

She is about to ask Paul if he knows the name of the loud, rollicking, catchy tune, when he extends a hand across the table. Palm up.

"Wanna dance?" he asks.

Diane looks at him warily, trying to remember the last time he asked her to dance. *Our wedding?*

Paul is *not* a dancer. And neither, truth be told, is Diane.

And yet. . . this music.

This. . . *song*.

Something about it makes her want to get up

and move to it, to hold her husband close and *dance* to it.

"Sure, why not?" she says, smiling.

But Paul's not smiling. Even as she places her hand in his and he squeezes it tight, he doesn't look happy, or eager.

He looks confused, she thinks, but then they're standing to follow the others toward the packed dance floor. Diane studies the empty tables as they pass by, turns and looks behind to see, to her shock, that *all* the tables are empty now.

Popular song, indeed.

They push themselves between other bodies, all of them swaying and bumping, a few clutched in shameless intimacy, a few dancing by themselves, swinging their hips, arms over their heads in what—at first—appears to be a sort of ecstasy. But as Diane studies the movements, they seem less fluid and more jarring; the couples' embraces less romantic, less sensual, and more desperate— the way one might cling to a loved one knowing the building around them is coming down, and there is nothing to do but wait for the inevitable.

After a few minutes, Diane grows tired. Her feet begin to ache, and she's lightheaded from the heat of the bar, the press of the bodies all around them. She studies Paul's face and notices that he's sweating and pale, his movements jerky and forced. The opposite of someone enjoying themselves.

"You want to sit?" she yells, the room booming with the song, now layered with the boisterous, raspy voice of a country rock singer belting out words and phrases that are meaningless to Diane's ears.

Paul looks at her and nods. "Yes, please."

She nods in return. . .

And they keep dancing.

A few moments pass. They look into each other's eyes. Paul's are wide and frightened, and Diane assumes hers must appear dreadfully similar.

"Paul?"

"I can't. . . can you stop?"

Diane shakes her head, looks around and sees that the others are watching them with strange looks on their faces.

Pity.

"What is this?" she yells. "Jesus, Paul!"

Diane is scared, bordering on hysterical. Suddenly she feels trapped in her own body, as if something else is in control of her movements, her actions, and she is nothing more than a spectator. She wants to scream, to run. . .

"Help us!" Paul yells, staring at each of the others surrounding them. But now those heated, sweating faces are turning away—not wanting to help, not wanting to see.

And still the music plays, roaring from the voracious, lustrous jukebox, and the heat of the room grows suffocating—bodies jostle and bump into each other, into Diane, and she begins to pray that she will simply faint away, that this is all a bad dream, that it can't possibly be happening. . .

And then she screams. Screams in horror, in frustration, in fear. And Paul yells at the others for help, to for God's sakes *help them*. Hearing his pleas, Diane could swear— at that exact moment —the music from the jukebox grows *louder*.

As if it's enjoying this.

As if *it* is the one in control.

Chapter Four

IT FEELS like hours later before the music finally, mercifully, stops.

A new, slower (and much quieter) song comes on and the forty-three souls in Happy's Bar and Grill collapse to the floor—some moaning, some crying—most silent but for their fast, heavy breaths.

After a few minutes, Paul and Diane, along with many others, crawl or stumble back to their seats, where they guzzle the water they'd placed there, wipe sweat from their faces with napkins, and rest their aching feet. Many folks put their heads on the tables, craving a nap. Some are already snoring.

Diane gulps down her water greedily, watches Paul do the same. She recalls the bartender's comment about getting the next round themselves and promises herself she'll refill their glasses after she has a moment to recover, to slow her heart.

"Paul?"

He holds up a finger as he drinks, hot breath steaming the inside of the emptying glass. He sets it down, shakes his head. "What the hell is this?" he mumbles, eyes wide and frantic, his face strained in a way Diane has never seen before.

Diane glances around the room, raises her voice. "Can someone help us? Can one of you just please explain?"

An older man two tables over looks her way. "You think we know, lady? Some of us been here for days. Hell, no one knows. . ."

"Oh, shut up, Lloyd!" a woman says from a table to Diane's left. "We all know what this is. At least," she ventures, doing a quick study of the faces around her, "most of us do. The ones who were here."

The older man—Lloyd—half stands before wincing and sitting back down. "Superstition!" he yells, face reddening, teeth bared. "Bullshit, I say!"

"Then how do you explain what's happening?" a young woman yells from a booth against the far wall, tears streaming down her face. "It's got to be what we did. It's got to be *her* doing this!"

More voices rise—some angry, some petulant, some confused as to what folks are talking about. Diane forces herself to stand, ignoring the protest of her cramping thighs. She turns her attention to the first woman. "Tell us what you mean, please. What happened here?"

Suddenly, the rising din of the room lessens, but more than one hard stare is aimed at the woman.

Threatening stares, Diane thinks.

"Please," Diane repeats.

"Shut your mouth, Maggie. . ." Happy pipes up from behind the bar, but his heart doesn't seem to be in it. By the looks of him, he's more worn out than anyone. "Don't say another word." He grips the edge of the bar so tight his knuckles turn white.

"I will not shut my mouth," Maggie says, then turns toward Diane. "I think we're being haunted," she says. "That's what all this is about. A haunting."

"Jesus, Mary, and Joseph," Lloyd grumbles.

"What do you mean, haunted?" Diane asks. "By who?"

Maggie, despite her frazzled hair and the streak of mascara running down one cheek, stares Diane square in the eye with a look of stone-cold sanity. "By the woman who was murdered here, on that very dance floor, one week ago."

Nearby, a tall, skinny man in a gray flannel shirt and jeans stands up, anger brewing in his eyes, looking like he means to repeat the bartender's threat. But the large man, the one with the python arms and black T-shirt, also stands, glaring nails at the first. "Let her finish. Enough is enough."

Maggie watches all this passively, then simply nods and looks back at Diane, although her determination seems to have wavered.

"Go on," Diane says, urging her on. "You said a woman was murdered?"

"Yes. . . yes, that's right," Maggie says. "Right there on that dance floor. A lot of us were here that night. We all saw it happen. In a way, I guess you could say we were. . . well. . . complicit."

Diane looks to Paul, who shrugs. She waits for someone to interrupt, to halt this confession. . . but no one says a word. She focuses on Maggie. "Complicit how?" she asks.

Maggie swallows hard and, when she finally speaks, her voice is hardly a whisper. "Because we covered it up, God help us," she says, eyes welling with tears. "We hid that poor girl's body."

Diane goes cold. "Hid her body where, Maggie?"

The older woman looks toward the jukebox. "Right there, lady. We hid her right over there."

Diane looks toward the dance floor, where the jukebox now plays a soft country song. "You mean. . ."

"That's right," Maggie says, wet lips trembling. "We buried that poor girl beneath the dance floor," she says, voice choked. She forces herself to stand, then points a finger toward the jukebox as tears stream down her cheeks. "And now that bitch is having her revenge, you see? She's having her revenge on all of us!"

Chapter Five

"I THINK I CAN HELP."

Diane had spoken with her husband in hushed tones while the room erupted in accusations and arguments, while some of the newcomers—trapped in the web which had been woven by a portion of the group—demanded answers. A few folks yelled and pointed at the others, demanding to know details of what had happened to the woman who, it was quickly revealed, was a twenty-two-year-old waitress named Sally Turner.

Other details made their way around the room as things grew heated: Sally had no family in the area, and few friends. She'd lived in a trailer a mile down the road, one she apparently inherited from a dead grandmother.

As the tinted bar windows slowly turned a brighter shade of gray, touched by a new day's morning sun, even more gruesome details emerged.

Sally had been dating a man named Elroy Jacobs, a known drunk and ruffian who worked as a part-time mechanic in the nearby town. Elroy had knocked Sally up, and on the night of the incident she'd been swollen with child.

"She was eight months and pretty as a ripe pear," a stern-looking woman had offered, as bits and pieces of the story filtered throughout the bar.

One night, as he often did, Elroy visited Sally at Happy's Bar and Grill, demanding free drinks and threatening to fight anyone who looked at him or Sally in a way he didn't like. Sally had just worked an eight-hour shift and was dead on her feet, but Elroy made her stay at the bar, made her dance with him despite her tiredness, despite the weight of carrying their child.

It was then that a fight broke out. Whether Elroy started it, or someone else was responsible, seemed to be a point of dispute among those who'd been in attendance, but a fight it was, nonetheless.

A fight on the dance floor.

More than just a fight. . . a *brawl*.

"I swear I saw a chair flying at one point," a bald man exclaimed, his neck long as a goose. "Worst damn fight I ever seen."

It was during the fight that Sally had been knocked to the ground.

It was during the fight that poor, pregnant Sally had been stepped on, again. . . and again. . . as she fought and crawled to escape, to find salvation. But bodies fell on top of her, crushed her to the floor, crushed her baby beneath her. She was savagely kicked in the head, her throat stomped by a steel-toed boot, breaking her neck.

It wasn't until someone started to scream—Maggie herself, perhaps—that everyone began to pull bodies apart, that bloodied and bruised men and women turned to stare at the cause of that horrible, blood-curdling shriek. . .

And saw Sally.

After a few hectic moments, it became obvious to everyone in the room that she was dead, and her unborn baby right along with her.

There were just shy of thirty people in the bar that night, half of whom had been dancing when the fight broke out, and any one of them could have trampled young Sally and her baby. Any one of them could be held complicit in her death.

"It was a couple of the women who suggested it first," Happy muttered, adding to the group's sad tale, his protestations forgotten now that it was all coming out, now that they were all in it together. "They didn't want their husbands in trouble. Some of these men," Happy said, eyeballing the group, "got police records. A couple are on probation."

And so, they buried her.

They locked the front door and pulled up a portion of the dance floor, beneath which Happy knew of a crawlspace he'd planked over when he remodeled the place more than a decade past. "Runs out to storm doors set into the ground out back, likely an old Prohibition tunnel," he said. "We pulled some sheets of plastic I keep around to cover the kegs I store outside, wrapped her up airtight, and laid her to rest."

After the group had replaced the floor, it was as if nothing had happened.

Aside from some blood, of course, which had been quickly mopped up. And some guilt, which was reasoned away; or, at the least, buried deeper than Sally.

"When we were done, when. . . when it was over, we tried to leave," Maggie says. "But the door wouldn't open. . . it wouldn't budge. None of the doors would open." She leans in close to Diane, voice low with terror. "The worst part was. . . after a few minutes of being locked in here? I swear, it was like we didn't *want* to leave. We all just sat down at these tables, settled in like it made all sorts of sense."

"And then that song came on," Lloyd says loudly. "That damned song!"

Maggie nods. "And we danced. Danced and danced..."

"Not to state the obvious," Paul says, trying to take it all in. "But have you tried just unplugging the damn thing? Or putting a chair through it?"

"Jukebox hasn't been plugged in for days," Happy mumbles from somewhere behind him. "Hell, I threw all the breakers just to be sure." Paul turns to see Happy staring up at the old-timey chandeliers, his face waxen and pale. "Whatever's fueling this place... it's ain't the power company. And it ain't natural."

"Over the past week, more folks have shown up," the big man adds (whose name, it turns out, is Max), pulling Paul's attention back. "And they stayed, just like all of us. Just like you." He spreads his thick arms wide, his face a grimace of shame and defeat. "And here we are."

"And what about this... Elroy?" Diane asks.

Heads turn toward the tall, skinny man in the gray flannel. The one she'd seen with rage burning in his brown eyes. He glares back at them all, then at Diane.

"I ain't done shit," he says. "This ain't on me."

"Take it easy, El," Max growls, and Diane

thanks the stars there's someone around to keep the obviously dangerous man under control.

It's then that Paul reaches out across the table and grips Diane's hand, an unspoken question in his eyes.

She knows what he wants of her.

And she knows she will have to try.

So Diane stands, and she tells the people trapped inside Happy's Bar and Grill that she's had some prior experience as a sensitive.

A medium.

That she has, in the past, communicated with the spirit realm.

That she can, potentially, reach out to the spirit of the dead girl.

That she can help.

Chapter Six

AFTER GENERAL AGREEMENT from the group that
Diane should try her ("hocus pocus bullshit" –
Lloyd / "liberal voodoo" – Happy) skills at
contacting the angry spirit, she barely has time to
formulate a plan before *that song* cranks out of the
jukebox once more, and once more everyone
stands—zombie-like—and shuffles to the dance
floor.

"Oh, God, so soon!" Maggie wails, miserably
breaking into a tired two-step.

Diane grips Paul tight as they step into the
group, then twists and shimmies to the music,
fighting the immediate press of exhaustion and

surge of nausea attacking her gut. To distract herself, she glances around until she spots Max, who's dancing in a sort of solo cowboy shuffle, thumbs jammed into belt loops, boots tapping almost gracefully against the floor.

"Move with me," she says to Paul, who only nods compliantly, sweat already matting his hair, his eyes slightly sunken and vacant.

Stay with me, hubby.

Moving her body to the impossibly loud, bass-thumping, window-rattling music, Diane forces her way through the throng toward the large man, pushing through the cramp of compressed flesh, the bodies of the others pumping and swirling around like an organic engine of madness.

When she's close to Max, she calls out to him and he looks up, catches her eye. She can't help notice a flash of embarrassment on that rough-ened—but handsome—face, as if he isn't one to normally dance in public, or at least not so vigor-ously. And likely never alone.

"Where is she?" Diane yells, ignoring the heads turning in her peripheral vision, most of the nearby dancers now watching her, watching Max.

Max stares back for a moment, as if debating, then his face falls, and he nods. He begins shuf-fling toward the far edge of the dance floor, the area closest to the hallway leading to the bath-rooms and fire exit.

Diane and Paul follow, and for the most part

the others move aside, understanding the goal. Some, however, throw a subtle elbow into her back, or tug violently at her hair. Behind her, she hears Paul exchange angry words with someone, but still she follows Max, needing to know...

Needing to see.

Max settles on a section of floor that is nearly seamless with the rest, but as he taps his boot heels and turns in circles, eyes wide and terrified, Diane can make out the seams where the smooth planks might have recently separated.

She sniffs the air, wondering if she'll smell decay, but within the mass of odorous, gyrating bodies all she gets is a whiff of body odor laced with an undercurrent of stale beer.

Diane looks at Paul meaningfully, clutches his hands in hers.

She closes her eyes for a moment, tries to open her mind, expand those extrasensory doorways that have allowed her to commune with the dead in the past.

Years ago, when she and Paul were in college, she'd hold séances with kids who'd lost parents, or siblings, or other loved ones. More times than not she could contact those spirits, let them talk *through* her while her own spirit slipped away, hovered above the scene while still tethered to her body, watched her own lips move with the words of the visiting entity. The others gasped and cried. Some ran from the room screaming.

When they were older, Diane moved away from her work as a medium, desiring a more normal life in which she and Paul could have children and a home, hold jobs that would not attract the wrong kind of attention, or make them oddities to neighbors or new friends.

So, she'd buried her secret, much like these people buried this poor woman. Stuffed it in a dark hole and covered it up, pretended it didn't exist.

But it does.

Now, as she dances, eyes closed, fingers intertwined with her husband's, she reaches out and—almost immediately and with a force she'd never experienced—*feels* the dead woman's spirit, and then some.

Rage.

Hate.

REVENGE.

But there is something else. . . . something Diane can't put her finger on. Beneath all those human emotions. . . there's something harder for her to define. A raw *need*. But still, the message is clear.

The spirit wants them to *stay*.

It wants them to *dance*.

Diane opens her eyes, fighting another wave of nausea.

"Well?" Paul says, looking more scared than she's ever seen him.

Diane lays her head against his chest, feels the sweat and heat of him. The comfort of him. "She's here, alright," she says, and then he pushes her gently away, spins her.

When she's facing him again, she looks into his eyes, her own terror now matching his. "And she's pissed."

Chapter Seven

AT THE TABLES, folks are sweating, breathless.

The tinted windows have darkened once more to an opaque black, a new night having crept its way to the front porch of Happy's Bar and Grill and settled over it—over all of them—like a cloud of death.

There's a line at the bar where Happy, despite his comments about everyone helping themselves, is filling waters from a soda gun as fast as he's able. Diane notices he's also handing out packets of peanuts and saltines, and feels her stomach grumble.

She ignores the discomfort, steadies her breath. She gets the feeling things are accelerating here and, perhaps, heading toward a disastrous end. Some of the locals have mentioned how, those first couple days, they'd only danced once or twice, then it became every five or six hours. . . and now?

Now it feels like it could happen any minute.

"I'm going to try and reach her," Diane says. "Paul, you need to communicate with her, understand? You need to talk to her and find a way to release us, release these people. Do it just like we did it in college, remember?"

Paul nods, swallows. "Yeah, okay. I think. . ." He looks around at the faces watching them. "I'll need help. At least two others."

Max stands from his chair like a rising mountain and walks over, sits down heavily at their table. A moment later, Maggie joins them on the opposite side.

Aside from a sad, soft country song leaking from the seemingly satiated jukebox, the bar has gone silent.

"Okay. . ." Diane says. "Hold hands, please. Form a conduit, if that makes sense."

Paul, Max, and Maggie hold hands, and Diane closes the connection.

"If this works, it won't be me you're speaking with, but Sally Turner."

"How will we know?" Max asks.

Diane smiles sadly, but her eyes are livid with fear. "You'll know."

As everyone watches, Diane closes her eyes, takes long, deep breaths. She doesn't speak or call out. There are no lit candles or crystal balls. There is the music, the ripe stench of fear, and the muddled orange lights of a dusty roadside bar in the middle of nowhere, trapped inside a world of horror.

After a few moments, Elroy stands from a few tables over, hands on hips, as if about to speak, to call bullshit on it all. . .

When Diane's eyes open.

Max winces as her fingers *squeeze*. Maggie cries out in pain as Diane grins, wider. . . wider. . . her eyes large and dark and blazing with hate.

"Keep the connection!" Paul says, gripping the hands of the two strangers on either side of him. Then he looks to his wife, to the spirit that wears her face like a mask.

"Who are you?" he says. "What's your name?"

Diane looks around, face flushed red, eyes unblinking, showing teeth. The people she looks at turn away. Cower. Hide from that stare.

She turns back to Paul. When she speaks, her voice is a higher pitch than Diane's, and it twangs with a light, southern lilt. "I'm Sally."

"Sally Turner," Paul says quietly, confirming.

Diane's dark eyes light up. "Hey, you're handsome. You wanna dance?"

Paul shakes his head. "Not yet, okay? I know you're angry, that you're hurt, that something horrible happened to you here. But please, most of us are strangers to you, to this place. Why keep us trapped? Why not let these people go?"

Diane's grin vanishes and she shakes her head violently. A moan slips from her mouth, a spill of drool runs down her chin and tears spring from the corners of her eyes. "NO NO NO!" she yells. "The folks in here got it coming for what they did." She slows her head, takes a few deep, raspy breaths. Her unfocused eyes roam the walls, the ceiling.

"Besides," she says, with a hint of mischief. "I like the company."

Paul shifts in his chair, thinking. "I understand, Sally. But we have homes and families. Many of us are innocent."

Diane stares at him a moment, eyes narrowing. "But not all of you," she says.

Her head turns to look at someone beside her, then keeps turning. Paul gasps when he hears a thin *snap* from his wife's neck. Finally, her gaze appears to settle on Elroy, who is still standing just behind them, a blank expression on his face.

"Not him," she says.

"Please, look back at me, Sally. Look over here, please. . ." Paul begs, and Diane's head turns back slowly, and Paul prays his wife hasn't been badly injured.

"Just tell me," he says. "What can we do? We'll do anything you want. . . if you'll just let us leave. We'll move your body, bury you properly, at a church, or a cemetery. But you have to open these doors, Sally. You must let us *out*."

"I'll tell you what," she says, grin widening once more. "I do have one idea. How about you and I have another dance, and I'll think on it."

"I. . ." Paul sputters, but then she's standing, hands pulled free from the others sitting at the table. She raises her arms above her head as if stretching, luxuriating in the new flesh. Then she cocks a hip seductively, and curls a finger at Paul.

"Come on, handsome," she says. "Let's dance!"

On cue, the jukebox *roars* the raucous song once more, the colored lights of its body glowing brighter, brighter, until it seems like the cursed machine may blast apart in a shower of glass and metal that would slice through the patrons like bullet shards.

Shouts of despair fill the room as everyone stands and makes their way to the dance floor, all of them shabby and spent, terrified beyond reason. Some are screaming for help, some are begging for it *to just stop*. Paul sees a few people collapse to the floor, only to emerge on hands and knees from beneath tables, doing whatever they can to make their way toward the fiendish jukebox.

Diane grabs Paul's hand and yanks him

forward, all but running for the far side of the bar. "Let's go, hot stuff!" she shrieks. "I got big plans for you!"

"Please, my wife!" Paul yells, not knowing what else to do, what's happening, or how to break the spell of the trance. *Or is it possession?* he thinks, mind racing. *Is Diane hovering over us even now, desperately trying to will her spirit back into the flesh?*

By the time Paul reaches the dance floor, the music is impossibly loud. Diane grips his hands with a strength he didn't think her capable of, his knuckles cracking under the pressure as his possessed wife begins flinging her body around in a jerky, clumsy rendition of a swing dance.

"Woohoo! Baby, you move divine!" she yells, then laughs as others crowd in around them, all of them shuffling their feet in a depressing approximation of moving with the music. Many are weeping openly now, and Paul sees one young man slapping himself in the face, over and over, as if trying to wake himself from a nightmare.

"Okay, Sally," he says, panting. One of his thighs tightens into a painful cramp and he winces, pain blasting up his leg, but still his body doesn't relent. "We're. . . we're dancing. . . now what were you going to tell me? What's your idea?"

Paul's wife looks at him in a way the real Diane never has. Never would. Her face tilts downward, eyes turned up toward him with devious intent, her smile stretched so wide it's cracked her upper lip. He stares at a small drop of blood resting there and prays for this all to be over.

"Promise you won't get mad, babyluv," she says, the twang in her voice growing more obvious, as if Sally was taking over more and more of Diane's body—her vocal cords, her tongue. Her mind. "But I'm gonna play the field for a bit. You're handsome and all, but this hot body? Good lord, man, it's crying out for attention. For, you know. . . *satisfaction*." She grips Paul by the back of the neck, thrusts her face to his and kisses him. He tastes the blood of her cracked lip as Diane's tongue plunges into his mouth.

When she pulls away, that devilish grin has turned into a pout, but her eyes shine with malice. "Don't worry, I'll be back. You just have fun!"

"Wait. . ."

But then she's gone, spinning away.

Paul watches with a mixture of horror and reflexive, jealous anger as his wife falls into the open arms of another man. The man, to his credit, looks to Paul with fear and wild eyes, as if saying: *It ain't me, brother! It ain't me!*

As he looks on, Diane presses herself against the man, then turns and forces her backside into his crotch and grinds her hips, pulls his hands around her waist and holds them there, all the while grinning at Paul, enjoying his impotent rage.

"Stop it!" he yells, trying to jostle his way toward her, to pull her away. "Stop it right now, goddammit!"

But Diane just shakes her head, spins around, and whispers something into the other man's ear. The stranger's eyes dart to Paul, then move across the dance floor.

As if searching for something, or someone.

Just as Paul is about to reach her, Diane darts away once more, laughing. Moments later he spots her, repeating the performance, this time with Max. The large man towers over her, disgust on his face.

Paul watches his wife press her mouth to Max's ear as well, lips moving rapidly against his ear.

When she pulls back, Max repeats the motion of the last man, looking around the dance floor at the faces surrounding them.

Searching.

Diane grips Max's face between her hands, pulls him down and kisses him on the mouth. Then she's off, moving to another, and another.

Paul desperately tries to reach her, to make his way through the hot, pressing bodies, but it's quickly become a lost cause. She's already made her way to more of the men, and it's only now Paul notices that those she's whispered to have all begun moving in the same direction—toward one point on the dance floor—as if they were a pack of hungry jackals closing in on weak prey.

He shoves his way between a young couple, desperate to see where the men are going. He bumps hard into someone and turns to see Maggie, who isn't so much dancing as shuffling her bare feet up and down.

"Maggie?"

She looks up at him with dead eyes, starts to speak, then collapses. Paul, his legs refusing to be still, awkwardly bends down, swipes at her shoulders, hoping to lift her...

A foot stomps on one of Maggie's outstretched hands. There's the audible snap of bone and she cries out. Suddenly, she's twisting her body to look upward; wild, terrified eyes settle on Paul, and he has a vision of what Sally might have looked like on that fateful night, crushed between jostling bodies, beaten to a painful, horrific death.

"Help me!" Maggie yells, but then a push of legs hits her like a wave and she's rolling over, crying out again and again for help, for the people hurting her to *stop*.

Before Paul can move toward her, another scream splits the air, rising like a siren above the sound of the roaring song. Paul looks toward the scream and sees a congregation of half a dozen men surrounding someone.

Elroy.

From one second to the next, chaos breaks out as the men attack. Max throws wild, giant fists toward Elroy's head, which the smaller man does his best to deflect with crossed arms. But now the others move in, punching at his head, kicking at his legs.

Paul notices Happy approaching from behind, grim determination on his face, and catches the briefest glint of something metal in the bartender's hand.

Is that. . . Jesus, is that a knife?

And then Elroy is shrieking in pain as Happy stabs the blade into his back again, and again, and again.

"Stop. . ." Paul says weakly, because now other bodies are pushing past him, more of the dancers trying to get to the spot where Elroy is being viciously, mercilessly murdered, wanting to end this once and for all. Wanting to *help*.

After a few moments, Elroy vanishes beneath the swarm of people, each of them desperate to get their pound of flesh so they can. . .

What? Paul thinks. *Be free? Is this the deal Sally has offered?*

If Elroy is indeed dead, or dying, beneath that tumult of rage. . .

Would they now be released?

Before he can think any further, a hand grips his from behind, spins him around. Diane's arms circle his waist. Her face stares up into his, and he notices that her lipstick is smeared, her hair wild.

Her blouse has been torn, revealing a bare shoulder, the black strap of her bra, the swell of a breast.

"Diane?"

She laughs and presses against him. His body, still out of his control, responds automatically as they move as one around the dance floor. As he dances, Paul feels something sticking to the bottom of his shoes and looks down, unsurprised to see a growing pool of blood beneath his feet.

A few others have begun screaming now, and he wonders numbly if the folks here have gotten a taste for murder. He thinks about Maggie being trampled, carried away from the torrent of moving bodies, the snap of the bone breaking in her hand.

Is this Maggie's blood I'm dancing in? Or Elroy's? Or someone else's altogether?

"Sally, you have what you want," Paul says, beyond exhaustion, beyond hope. He gazes deep into his wife's brown eyes, searching for a spark of her soul, of her mind. "Elroy's dead. . . my God, people are dying. You *must* let us go now. You need to stop the music and let us go."

"I've decided that I like you!" she says loudly, ignoring his pleas. She tries to kiss him once more, but he shoves her away. She stumbles, catches her balance, then grins at him. "Don't be mean, now, or I won't dance with you no more."

Before he can reply, she lunges at him with a wild laugh, grips him tight around the waist. All around them is blood and chaos, screams and terror and murder.

"This was your idea, right?" he asks. "To kill Elroy, the one who started all of this? So please, I'm begging you. . . give me my wife back. Let us go home."

Diane's grin falters a moment, and her eyes study Paul closely. "Honeybear, what makes you think I'm the one in charge here?"

Paul's flesh goes cold, his eyes widen. He stares into the face of his wife, which looks less and less like Diane with each moment that passes.

"What the hell does that mean?"

Sally *(for it is Sally,* he thinks. . . *it's all Sally now)* laughs again, then hoots and slaps him in the chest. "God, I sure love dancing with you," she says. "I could dance with you forever. And he sure can pick 'em, can't he?"

Paul looks toward the jukebox, now just a few feet away, vibrating with the beats of the music, a rainbow of colors bursting from inside the machine that seems to have come alive, fueled by a raging *joy*. A great pulsing heart bursting with madness.

"What the hell are you talking about?" Paul says, the words like ash on his tongue as he tries to desperately hold onto the fraying threads of logic, of his sanity. "Who can pick 'em?"

Sally looks at him with a furrowed brow, as if wondering how just how goddamn stupid some people could be. "Who you thinks been playing these songs?" she says. "He's doing it right now, whipping out the hits!"

Paul grips her arms hard, but she only smiles up at him, eyes blazing with a manic, wild glee.

"Who?" he yells, ignoring the squelch of something fleshy beneath one heel as his feet continue stomping in a hellish rhythm with the music.

"My baby, that's who," Sally says, pressing herself into Paul, her body hot and fluid as melted steel. She points toward the jukebox—which continues pulsing with demonic, tireless pleasure —an elated smile on her lips.

"That's my baby boy in there," she says proudly, her shrill voice carrying above the rising tumult of death and music. "Ain't he something?!"

ABOUT THE AUTHOR

Philip Fracassi is the author of the novels *A Child Alone with Strangers, Gothic, Boys in the Valley, The Third Rule of Time Travel*, among others. *The New York Times* called his work "terrifically scary."

Philip lives in Los Angeles, California, and is represented by Elizabeth Copps at Copps Literary Services.

pfracassi.com

ALSO BY PHILIP FRACASSI

NOVELS

The Third Rule of Time Travel

Boys in the Valley

Gothic

A Child Alone with Strangers

Don't Let Them Get You Down

COLLECTIONS

No One is Safe

Beneath a Pale Sky

Behold the Void

NOVELLAS

Commodore

Shiloh

Sacculina

A NOTE FROM
SHORTWAVE PUBLISHING

Thank you for reading *D7*! If you enjoyed this book,
please consider writing a review. Reviews help readers
find more titles they may enjoy, and that helps us
continue to publish titles like this.

For more Shortwave titles, visit us online...

OUR WEBSITE

shortwavepublishing.com

SOCIAL MEDIA

@ShortwaveBooks

EMAIL US

contact@shortwavepublishing.com

www.ingramcontent.com/pod-product-compliance
Lightning Source LLC
LaVergne TN
LVHW031426130225
803500LV00006B/146